# THE AMAZING SPIDER-MAN™

# Becoming SPIDER-MAN

WRITTEN BY
**TOMAS PALACIOS**

BASED ON THE MOTION PICTURE SCREENPLAY WRITTEN BY
**JAMES VANDERBILT**

NEW YORK

Published by Marvel Press, an imprint of Disney Book Group. No part of this book may
be reproduced or transmitted in any form or by any means, electronic or mechanical,
including photocopying, recording, or by any information storage and retrieval system,
without written permission from the publisher. For information address Marvel Press,
114 Fifth Avenue, New York, New York 10011-5690.

Printed in the United States of America

First Edition

1 3 5 7 9 10 8 6 4 2

G658-7729-4-12106

ISBN 978-1-4231-5487-7

This is the story of Peter Parker and how he became the Amazing Spider-Man!

When Peter was a boy, he lived with his parents in a nice house.

He would play hide-and-seek in his dad's office.

The office was very strange and filled with old things.

One night, someone broke into Peter's dad's office.

This frightened Peter's parents.

Peter's parents had to protect him.

They took Peter to live with Aunt May and Uncle Ben.

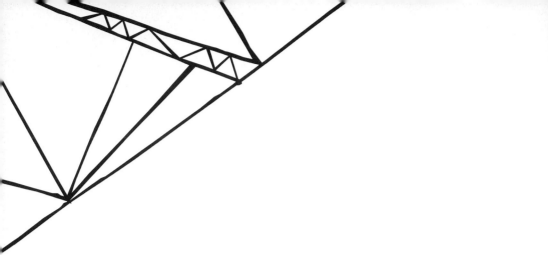

Ten years passed, and Peter was all grown up.

He was a teenager and went to high school.

Peter enjoyed science and taking pictures.

Peter was just another normal kid.

But that was about to change.

One day, Uncle Ben gave Peter
a briefcase that belonged to
Peter's father.

Inside was a picture of Peter's
dad standing with a man named
Dr. Connors.

Peter decided to find Dr.
Connors and ask about his dad.

Peter went to a lab called Oscorp. Dr. Connors worked there.

Peter spoke to Dr. Connors, but he wanted to learn more. So he decided to sneak around Oscorp and look for clues.

Peter came to a top secret lab and went inside.

Suddenly, a strange spider came down from the ceiling and bit Peter!

Peter was scared and ran out of the building.

But when he got on a train to go home, something strange happened!

The spider bite had given Peter Super Powers!

Peter got off the train and ran all the way home.

When he got there, he was very hungry.

Aunt May and Uncle Ben watched as Peter ate everything in the fridge!

Then Peter got very tired and went to bed.

The next day, Peter learned more about his new Super Powers.

He could climb walls.

He could run really fast.

Peter even had super strength!

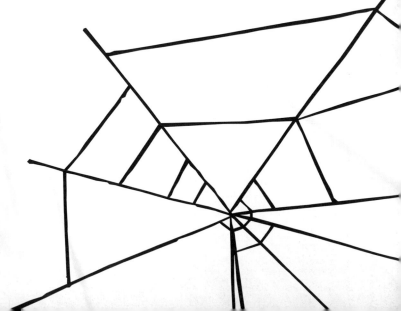

While out practicing with his new powers, Peter fell through a roof and landed in an old gym.

Inside, he saw a huge poster of a wrestler wearing a mask. That gave Peter an idea.

Peter needed to make a costume.

The next day, Peter went to
school.

He sat at his desk and began to
imagine his Super Hero costume.

He started to draw in his
notebook.

When he looked down, he had
drawn his Super Hero mask!

Peter's costume was almost
done!

Peter raced home and went to his room.

He began to work on his costume. He used red and blue cloth.

He sewed and sewed.

After a few hours, Peter was done!

It fit perfectly!

But something was still missing.

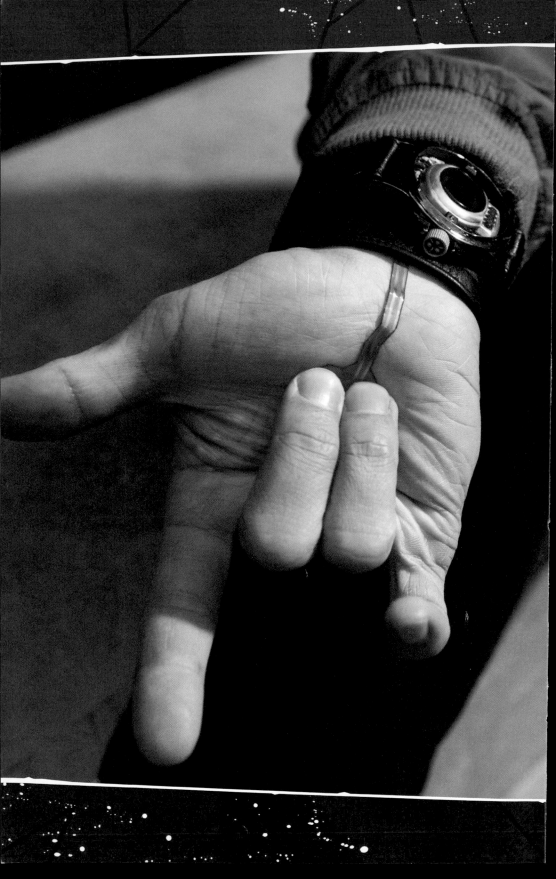

Peter needed something that would help him swing from building to building.

At Oscorp he found a special web fluid. It was very strong and very sticky.

He went home and made a web-shooter device.

Now he could spin a web— just like a spider!

Peter went out and tested his new costume and web-shooters. Peter swung through New York City.

He was a natural! He even stopped a car thief!

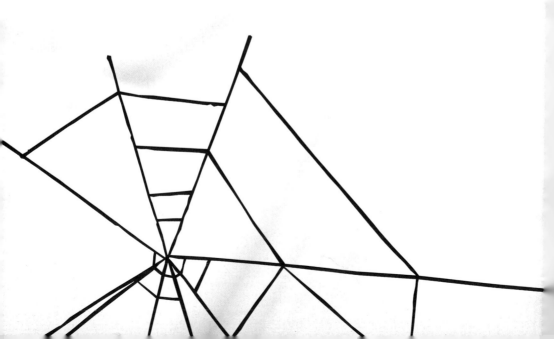

All Peter needed was a cool Super Hero name to go along with his costume.

And so he chose the Amazing Spider-Man!

Peter Parker had come a long way from being a kid in high school.

He was now a Super Hero with great powers . . . and a great responsibility to help others.

And Peter would do it as the Amazing Spider-Man!